This book belongs to:

_____

For Scout and Poppy
with love

This paperback edition first published in 2015 by Andersen Press Ltd.

First published in Great Britain in 2014 by Andersen Press Ltd.,

20 Vauxhall Bridge Road, London SW1V 2SA.

Published in Australia by Random House Australia Pty.,

Level 3, 100 Pacific Highway, North Sydney, NSW 2060.

Copyright © Michael Foreman, 2014.

The rights of Michael Foreman to be identified as the author and illustrator

of this work have been asserted by him in accordance with

the Copyright, Designs and Patents Act, 1988.

All rights reserved. Printed and bound in Malaysia by Tien Wah Press.

1 3 5 7 9 10 8 6 4 2

British Library Cataloguing in Publication Data available.

ISBN 978 1 78344 165 5

CAT & DOG

MICHAEL FOREMAN

ANDERSEN PRESS

It was a wet and
windy night.

Cat found a dry place
under the bridge and
hugged her kittens to
keep them warm.

In the morning, Cat sniffed the air. Her nose twitched.
"Fish! I smell fish," she said. "Stay here, my dears.
I'll be back soon with breakfast."

The kittens watched Cat follow the fishy smell up to the busy street. She stopped beside a parked van, sniffed the air again and then jumped in through the open door.

SLAM! Moments later the door shut behind her, the engine started and the van drove off!

"Mum! Come back!" the kittens cried in alarm, but the van had disappeared in the traffic and the kittens were left all alone.

They huddled together to keep warm and
watched and waited for the van to return.

As it grew dark, a scruffy old dog wandered under
the bridge, looking for somewhere dry to sleep.

The dog saw the three kittens.
"Breakfast, lunch and dinner," he thought,
licking his lips.

Then he thought again. "Poor little things. They
seem to be alone in the world, like me."

The old dog curled up on some potato sacks and went to sleep.
He had a lovely dream…
He was being stroked and tickled.

He opened one eye.
"Oh, you're so warm," one of the kittens said.
"Can we warm ourselves next to you?"
The old dog sighed and wrapped his tail around them.

"Breakfast!" the dog said when he woke them up in the morning.

All day the kittens watched the busy road, hoping that Mum would come back. The dog made sure no other dogs or foxes came near.

Then, at last, there
was the van!
The driver got out,
carrying Cat.

He put her gently on
the ground. Cat raced
towards the kittens.

They rolled and cuddled and licked and kissed.

Suddenly, Cat saw the dog. She arched her back, showed all her teeth and claws and hissed at him.

"No, Mum! He is our friend!" the kittens cried.
"He looked after us."

The old dog backed away, sat down and listened as Cat told them of her adventure.

"It was awful in the back of the van, cold and dark and bumpy," she said. "We went all the way to the seaside! The man was so surprised to see me when he opened the door, but he was very kind and warmed me up and gave me a fish supper.

But, I couldn't eat it – I was too worried about all of you.

Then he told me to eat up.
'I have to deliver some more fish to the city tomorrow and
I will take you back with me,' he said."

Then Cat told them all about the seaside… the boats
and waves and fresh air. It sounded wonderful.

Dog and the kittens
wanted to see it for
themselves, so when the
driver came back to his
van, he found he had a
few extra passengers.

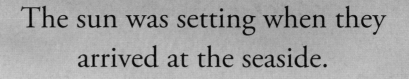

The sun was setting when they
arrived at the seaside.

The fish man made them at home
in his net shed by the harbour.

After supper they all walked to the end of
the pier by the light of the moon.

"There's a whole wonderful world out there," said Dog.
"Yes, and a sea full of fish," said Cat.

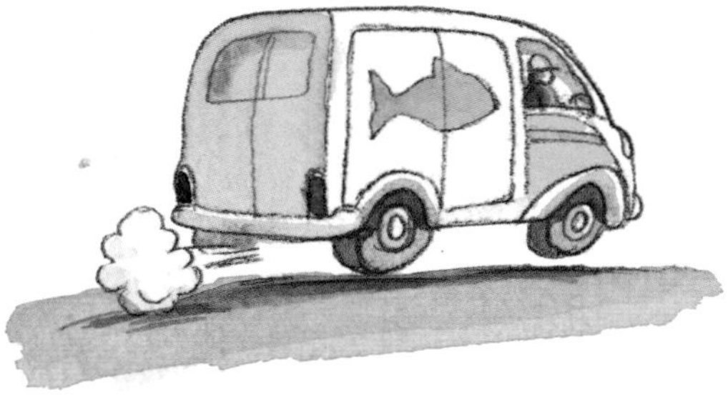